Tayra's Not Talking

To Vivian and Cienna — L.B.

To Estelle, a very creative and determined
young woman *qui va aller très loin*! — C.B.

Published in Canada and the U.S. by Kids Can Press Ltd.
25 Dockside Drive, Toronto, ON M5A 0B5

Kids Can Press is a Corus Entertainment Inc. company

www.kidscanpress.com

The artwork in this book was rendered by hand-drawing
and digital collage.
The text is set in Cabrito Didone.

Edited by Jennifer Stokes and Debbie Rogosin
Designed by Michael Reis

Printed and bound in Shenzhen, China, in 10/2021 by Imago

CM 22 0 9 8 7 6 5 4 3 2 1

Library and Archives Canada Cataloguing in Publication

Title: Tayra's not talking / written by Lana Button ; illustrated
by Christine Battuz.
Names: Button, Lana, 1968– author. | Battuz, Christine,
illustrator.
Identifiers: Canadiana 20210199954 | ISBN 9781525304842
(hardcover)
Classification: LCC PS8603.U87 T39 2022 | DDC jC813/.6 — dc23

Kids Can Press gratefully acknowledges that the land on
which our office is located is the traditional territory of
many nations, including the Mississaugas of the Credit, the
Anishnabeg, the Chippewa, the Haudenosaunee and the
Wendat peoples, and is now home to many diverse First
Nations, Inuit and Métis peoples.

We thank the Government of Ontario, through Ontario
Creates; the Ontario Arts Council; the Canada Council for
the Arts; and the Government of Canada for supporting our
publishing activity.

Tayra's Not Talking

Written by Lana Button & Illustrated by Christine Battuz

KIDS CAN PRESS

HI!

What's your name?

Sooooooo ...
how old are you?

This kid won't say a single word,
so now what do we do?

Let's talk a little **LOUDER** to her.
H–E–L–L–O–O–O–! CAN YOU HEAR?

Well, now she's looking grumpy
with a finger in each ear.

It's time for us to go inside.

We can't stay at the gate.

So get in line and follow us ...

Come on, or you'll be late.

The teacher asked her lots of things,
but all she did was *stare*!
Would *you* ignore Miss Seabrooke?!
I know *I* would never dare!

Is she being stubborn?

Is she being rude?

Is she just, on purpose, in some

I'm-not-talking mood?

RRRING!

There's the bell, so let's begin.
It's time to start our day.

Oh! You've had a tumble.
Hedgie, dear, are you okay?

I saw — that new kid pushed him!
She knocked him to the ground.
She *has* to say she's sorry,
but she *still* won't make a sound.

He didn't do a single thing
to make the new kid mad.
I wonder if she *likes* to push!
Do you think she's **bad**?

I can tell she's sorry.
I see it on her face.

Well, *you* play with her, Kitty.
But be careful — just in case!

A brand-new friend has just arrived
and joined our class today.
I'm sure you'll be excited
to include her in your play.

Help me welcome Tayra.

Hi there, Tayra.

Hello.

Hi!

Perhaps our friend is overwhelmed.
She could be feeling shy.

We'll give her time to settle in,
and soon she'll get to know us.

Though Tayra might not *tell* us things,
we'll watch — perhaps she'll *show* us.

I think if I were in her shoes,
and I was somewhere new,
I'd wish I had a friend around,
to show me what to do.

Like ... what if I was in a place
and couldn't let you know
that I can't find the bathroom,
but I really have to go!

And maybe I'd be cranky
if I *wished* that I could say,
I'm feeling really hungry,

or *that's* where I want to play.

We know that Tayra likes to draw,
and she has two big sisters.
She's sorry she knocked Hedgie down.
She told us with her pictures!

Guess what!? The ringing *scared* her!
She showed us with her hands.
So *we* showed her it's just the bell,
and now she understands!

Tayra isn't singing,
but she's grooving to this song.
Here, Tayra, grab an instrument.
We'll sing — you play along.

She's really great at dancing!
It sure looks fun to do!
Hey, Tayra, can you show us how,
so we can dance with you?

We thought that Tayra *had* to talk
before we all could play.
But we did lots of different things
and made a friend today!

And Tayra's looking happy, too.
We're glad she likes it here.
We know, because she told us ...

with her smile from ear to ear!